The Pug who wanted to be an Elf

Text by Anne Marie Ryan.

Illustrations by Nina Jones and Artful Doodlers.

ORCHARD BOOKS

First published in Great Britain in 2022 by Hodder & Stoughton

1 3 5 7 9 10 8 6 4 2

Text copyright © Hodder & Stoughton Ltd, 2022
Illustrations copyright © Hodder & Stoughton Ltd, 2022

A CIP catalogue record for this book
is available from the British Library.

ISBN 978 1 40836 503 8

Printed and bound in Great Britain by Clays Ltd, Elcograf S.p.A.
The paper and board used in this book are made from wood from responsible sources.

Orchard Books
An imprint of
Hachette Children's Group
Part of Hodder & Stoughton
Carmelite House
50 Victoria Embankment
London EC4Y 0DZ

An Hachette UK Company
www.hachette.co.uk
www.hachettechildrens.co.uk

The Pug who wanted to be an Elf

Bella Swift

Contents

Chapter One

Peggy the pug was sitting under a table at Pups and Cups café, watching customers and their dogs come in and out. It was a cold December day, so everyone was bundled up in coats and woolly hats and scarves. *Humans must get very chilly,* thought Peggy. She was glad that she had tan-coloured fur to keep her toasty warm in winter.

The café's radio was playing quietly in the background. "Stay tuned for a chance to win a trip to Lapland," said the radio presenter.

"Ooh," said Peggy's best friend, Chloe, who was sitting at the table doing her homework with her siblings. "We should enter the competition."

Chloe's older brother, Finn, looked up from his geography textbook and nodded. "It would be awesome to see the northern lights. We learned about them at school."

"And we could visit Santa's

workshop!" said their little sister, Ruby.

Their mum, who owned the café, came over to the table, holding a tray with three hot chocolates and a plate of gingerbread biscuits.

"Thanks, Mum" said Chloe, helping herself to a biscuit and dunking it in her hot chocolate.

"Hey! What about me?" asked Peggy. To her human friends, it just sounded like she was barking.

"Sorry, Peggy," said Mum. "I've sold out of my bacon and peanut butter dog treats." Pups and Cups was a dog-friendly café, selling tasty treats for dogs as well as snacks for humans.

Humph, thought Peggy, resting her head on her paws.

"Is Dad taking us to the park later?" asked Chloe.

Peggy's ears pricked up. She loved

going to the park!

"I'm afraid not, darling," said Mum. "He's working today. That's why you're here with me."

"But it's Saturday," grumbled Chloe.

"Dad's installing a new computer system for a big client," explained Mum.

That sounds fun, thought Peggy. She knew all about computers. She sometimes watched adorable puppy videos with Chloe.

"That's why he has to work over the weekend," continued Mum. "But hopefully he'll have done the work by Christmas."

The bell above the door jingled and

Sandy the post carrier came into the café. "Good morning!" she greeted them. She reached into her red bag and handed Mum her mail.

"Thanks, Sandy," said Mum, sorting through the envelopes.

"Hello, Peggy," said Sandy, crouching down to pat Peggy on the head.

Some dogs didn't like post carriers, but Peggy was

great friends with Sandy. She licked the post carrier's hand and wagged her curly little tail.

"How about a coffee?" offered Mum. "On the house."

"Ooh, that'd be lovely," said Sandy. She rubbed her hands together. "It's chilly out there today."

As Mum went behind the counter to make Sandy a hot drink, the post carrier turned to the children. "Have you written your letters to Santa?"

"Not yet," said Chloe.

"Well, don't leave it too long," said Sandy. "It takes a few days for a letter to get to him."

Mum handed the post carrier a steaming takeaway cup.

"Thank you!" said Sandy. Giving them a cheery wave, she left the café with her coffee, to continue on her route.

"Sandy's right, you know," said Mum. "You kids should write letters to Santa so the elves in his workshop know what toys to make for you."

"I'm too old for toys," said Finn, rolling his eyes. "I want new football boots and computer games."

Ruby tore a sheet of paper from her notebook, got a pencil out of her pencil case and began to write. Chloe took out a piece of paper as well. Chewing on the end of her pencil, she stared at the blank page as Ruby wrote her letter.

"How do you spell 'ice skates'?" Ruby asked, looking up.

Finn spelled the words out for her.

"How come you're not writing anything?" Ruby asked her sister.

Shrugging, Chloe picked Peggy up. "I just can't think of anything I want."

I know what I want . . . thought Peggy, drooling as she eyed the plate of gingerbread on the table. She whined hopefully as Chloe stroked her back.

"You could ask for new clothes," suggested Finn.

"Or some new books," called Mum from behind the counter. "You love reading."

"I'm asking for toys," said Ruby. She read out her letter:

Dear Santa,

I hope you and your elves are well. I have been a very good girl this year. Please will you bring me a teddy, a LEGO set, a new board game and a pair of ice skates.

Love,

Ruby

PS Finn wants football boots.

"That's great, Ruby," said Chloe, smiling at her little sister.

"If Santa brings me a new game we

can play it on Christmas Day," said
Ruby.

"That's what I love best about
Christmas," said Chloe. "Spending time
as a family."

"Yeah," agreed Finn. He paused. "But
I still want some new football boots."

Ruby took out
her crayons
and
decorated
her letter
with a
picture of
an elf and
some presents.

The song that was playing finished and the radio presenter said, "And now, as regular listeners will know, it's time for our Christmas competition . . ."

"Turn it up, Mum!" said Chloe.

Mum raised the volume.

"After the break, one lucky winner will win a family trip to Lapland if they answer three trivia questions correctly. To enter, call this number . . ."

As the presenter read out the number, Chloe scribbled it down on her piece of paper. "Quick! Call this number!" she said, running over to the counter to give it to her mum.

Mum wiped her hands on her apron,

then she took out her phone and keyed in the number. "It's ringing," she told the children.

They waited anxiously as adverts played on the radio.

"Welcome back to the show," said the presenter. "We have a lucky caller on the line. Can you tell our listeners your name?"

There was a pause, then Mum's eyes widened. "Oh! It's me!" she said. "I mean, Helen Williams."

Peggy's brow wrinkled in confusion. Mum's voice seemed to be coming from two places at the same time. How was that possible?

"Mum's on the radio!" gasped Chloe.

"Are you feeling lucky today, Helen?" asked the presenter.

Mum nodded.

"You've got to say something!" whispered Finn.

"Y-y-yes!" said Mum nervously. She came round the counter to the table where the children were sitting.

"OK, Helen," said the presenter smoothly. "You have one minute to answer three trivia questions correctly. If you get them all right, you and your family will be off on a dream holiday to Lapland. We'll start with an easy one: what are Santa's helpers called?"

"Err . . ." said Mum.

Ruby held up her letter to Santa and pointed frantically to the elf she'd drawn.

"Elves," said Mum into the phone.

"Correct!" said the presenter. "The next question is a bit harder: what is the aurora borealis?"

"Um . . ." said Mum.

Picking up his geography textbook, Finn quickly turned the pages until he found what he was looking for. He held up a picture in the book.

"The northern lights," said Mum.

"That's right!" said the presenter. "Now, if you can answer just one more question correctly, that holiday will be yours."

The children exchanged anxious looks. Mum swallowed nervously.

"*Piparkakku* is a sweet treat eaten in Lapland at Christmastime," said the presenter. "What do we call it in English?"

The radio played the sound of a ticking clock. Mum looked at the children but they all shrugged and shook their heads.

"Let me think . . ." said Mum.

"Think quickly," said the presenter, chuckling. "Because you've only got fifteen seconds left."

Peggy stared at the gingerbread on the table longingly. Nobody was paying any attention to her, so she decided to take her chances. She reached for the plate with her front paw, dragging it towards her. *Nearly got it,* thought Peggy as the plate slid closer and closer to the edge of the table—

"Gingerbread!" called Mum in warning. Chloe grabbed the plate of gingerbread biscuits just in the nick of time, stopping it from falling off the table.

"That's correct!" said the presenter. "*Piparkakku* is the Finnish word for gingerbread. Congratulations, Helen, you've just won yourself a family trip to Lapland!"

Chapter Two

"I can't believe we won a holiday!" said
Chloe as they walked home from the
café. Peggy was trotting along next to
her on her lead. Darkness had fallen
and Peggy liked looking at the bright
Christmas lights decorating the trees
and houses along the way.

"We very nearly didn't," said Mum, laughing. "I was so nervous about being on the radio my mind went completely blank."

"Thank goodness for Peggy!" said Chloe proudly. She had been so happy she'd given her a gingerbread biscuit as a treat. Peggy licked her chops, thinking of how tasty it had been.

"I can't wait to tell Dad that we're going to Lapland for Christmas," said Finn.

"He deserves a holiday," said Mum. "He's been working so hard."

"So do you, Mummy," said Ruby. "You deserve a holiday too."

When they reached their house, the lights were on. Dad had just got back from work. He opened the door, looking tired but happy to see them.

"Daddy! Daddy! Guess what?" said Ruby, running up to him. He picked her up and gave her a hug.

"We won a trip to Lapland!" said Finn.

"All because of Peggy!" added Chloe.

Dad gave Mum a confused look.

"It's true," she said, smiling. "We won a radio competition."

Finn hurried into the house and got his laptop. "Look!" he said, tapping on the keyboard and calling up pictures

of Lapland. They all gathered round
the kitchen table to look at the snowy
images. Peggy hopped up on Chloe's
lap to get a better view as Finn scrolled
through the pictures.

"We can see the northern lights!" Finn said, clicking on a picture of a night sky with green and purple lights dancing across it.

Oooh, thought Peggy. *Those are so pretty!*

"And go ice skating," said Chloe as Finn scrolled past an image of an ice rink.

"If we're lucky, we might even get to meet Santa!" said Ruby, pointing to a picture of a wooden chalet with a sign that read SANTA'S WORKSHOP.

"I expect Santa is pretty busy at this time of year," said Mum, laughing.

"Oh wow," said Dad, peering at the

screen. "Lapland looks amazing. But unfortunately, I won't be able to join you."

"What?" said Chloe.

Dad ran his hand through his curly hair. "There's a problem with the software. I'm probably going to need to work through Christmas to meet the deadline."

"Oh dear . . ." said Mum. "What a shame."

Poor Dad, thought Peggy. Lapland looked so beautiful.

"But the four of you must go," said Dad. "You'll have a wonderful adventure and you can tell me all about it when you get back."

"But it won't be the same without you," said Chloe. Her lip trembled and Peggy could tell that her best friend was on the brink of tears. That made Peggy want to cry too.

"Don't worry about me," said Dad, giving her a hug. "I'll have Peggy to keep me company."

Huh? thought Peggy, confused.

"Why wouldn't Peggy come with us?" asked Chloe. "We wouldn't have even won the competition without her."

"I'm not sure if dogs are allowed," said Dad.

Peggy whimpered sadly. She loved

Dad but hated the thought of being separated from Chloe – especially at Christmastime.

Chloe cuddled Peggy tight. "If Peggy isn't allowed to come, then I'm staying at home too!" she announced.

"Let me see what I can do." Mum went off to make a few telephone calls, and a while later she came back, smiling. "It's all fine," she said. "I spoke to the airline and sorted it out. Peggy is coming too!"

"Yippee!" barked Peggy, wagging her tail. She was going to Lapland!

"Can you believe we're flying to Lapland tomorrow morning?" asked Chloe as she pulled open a drawer and took out a pair of pyjamas.

Peggy glanced at herself in the mirror on the back of Chloe's wardrobe door. *Nope,* no signs of wings yet. Chloe hadn't sprouted any either. Peggy wasn't quite sure how they were going to fly to Lapland without wings. Hopefully they would grow overnight.

"It's really cold in Lapland," said Chloe, "so I need to pack lots of warm clothes." She opened another drawer and took out socks and thermal vests. Peggy watched as she added them to the purple suitcase on top of her bed.

Chloe stood with her hands on her hips, looking down at the overflowing suitcase. "Hmm. I'm not sure if I'm going to be able to shut it."

I can help, thought Peggy. She jumped up on the bed and climbed into the suitcase. She started squishing Chloe's clothes down with her paws.

"Silly Peggy," said Chloe, plucking her out of the suitcase. "You're getting dog hair all over my clothes."

"Did you pack your ice skates?" asked Dad, coming into Chloe's room.

Chloe's hands flew to her mouth. "Oh no! That's another thing I need to fit in." She went back to her wardrobe, took out a pair of white ice skates and added them to her suitcase.

"Take a break from packing and come downstairs," said Dad. "I want to give you something." He picked Peggy up. "You too, Pegs."

They went downstairs to the living room where the rest of the family were gathered by the Christmas tree, which sparkled with twinkling lights. There were five gift-wrapped presents under the tree.

"I thought I'd give you your gifts today," said Dad. "As I won't be with you on Christmas Day." He handed a present to everyone. There was even one for Peggy!

Mum and the children opened their gifts. They each contained a woolly jumper with a snowflake pattern on it.

"They'll keep you nice and warm in Lapland," said Dad.

"It's so soft," said Chloe, rubbing it against her cheek.

"And really cosy," said Mum. She gave
Dad a kiss.

"Thanks, Dad!" said Finn, pulling his
jumper over his head.

Ruby put on her sweater and held
her arm next to her brother's. "We all
match!" she said happily.

Peggy tugged at the ribbon on her

present with her teeth.

"Let me help," said Chloe. She untied the ribbon and tore off the wrapping paper. Inside the box was a red dog sweater with a green collar and a matching hat. "Aww! That's so cute! It's a little elf outfit."

Why would I need that? thought Peggy. *I've got fur to keep me warm.*

"Who wants to hear a Christmas story?" asked Dad.

"Me!" said Ruby. She got a picture book from the bookshelf and climbed on to his lap. Chloe and Peggy snuggled next to them. Even Finn listened.

The story was about an elf who went

out in a snowstorm to deliver a letter to Santa. It had a happy ending, and the girl who'd written the letter got the doll she wanted for Christmas – all thanks to the brave little elf.

"Have you written your letter to Santa yet?" Ruby asked Chloe.

"Not yet," she said.

"Time's running out," said Finn.

"Bedtime," said Mum. "We've got a big day tomorrow."

"Yay!" said Ruby, jumping up and down on the sofa excitedly. "We're going on holiday!"

"This time tomorrow, we'll be in Lapland!" said Finn.

Only Chloe didn't seem excited. Concerned, Peggy followed her friend as she trudged upstairs, changed into her pyjamas, then climbed into bed and got under the duvet. Peggy curled up next to her.

Before long, Dad came in to say goodnight.

"I wish you were coming with us, Dad," said Chloe.

"Me too, sweetpea," he said, giving Chloe a goodnight kiss. He patted Peggy, then switched off the bedroom light on his way out.

Chloe tossed and turned in bed. Finally, she got out of bed and tiptoed across the room. Peggy sat up on her haunches and watched as her friend got out a sheet of paper from her desk. Moonlight streamed in through the window, bathing Chloe in its silvery glow as she began to write.

What she's writing? wondered Peggy. Was it a last-minute packing list?

Finally, Chloe set her pencil down and read her letter to Peggy in a whisper:

Dear Santa,

Happy Christmas. I don't need any toys this year. All I want is for my dad to be with us.

Lots of love,

Chloe xxx

Chloe folded the letter and set it on her bedside table. Then she climbed back into bed and pulled the covers up to her chin. "Night night, Peggy," she said.

Soon, Chloe was fast asleep. Listening to her friend's soft snores, Peggy glanced over at the letter. *Will it get to Santa before Christmas?* she worried.

She hoped with all her heart it would arrive in time. She couldn't bear the thought of her friend being sad on Christmas Day.

Chapter Three

It was still dark when Chloe's alarm clock woke them up at dawn the next morning. Chloe hopped out of bed, but Peggy crawled under the duvet where it was nice and warm.

"Get up, Peggy," said Chloe, putting on jeans and her new snowflake jumper.

"We can't be late for our flight."

Peggy yawned and reluctantly got out of bed, stretching her short legs behind her.

"Let's get you dressed too," said Chloe, pulling Peggy's new red sweater over her head. Peggy tried to wriggle away, but Chloe wouldn't let her escape. "You'll thank me when we get to Lapland. It's much colder there," she said.

44

Then she put the hat on Peggy's head.

I feel ridiculous, thought Peggy, trying to shake it off.

After packing her toothbrush and a few other last-minute things, Chloe zipped up her suitcase and lugged it downstairs, where the others were waiting.

"Aww!" said Ruby as they came down the stairs. "Peggy looks so cute."

"Do you have everything you need?" asked Dad.

Mum pulled a checklist out of her purse. "Suitcases . . . tickets . . . money . . . passports . . ." she read.

"We're going to see Santa!" sang

Ruby, dancing around the hallway.

Santa! thought Peggy. She suddenly remembered something Chloe had forgotten to pack – her letter to Santa! She bounded up the stairs.

"Come back, Peggy," called Chloe, chasing after her.

Peggy dashed into Chloe's bedroom and grabbed the letter in her mouth. She tucked it under her jumper for safekeeping. There was no guarantee that they would meet Santa in Lapland, so she would look out for a postbox to drop it in to.

"There you are," said Chloe, clipping on Peggy's lead. "We've got to go now."

They packed the suitcases into the boot and climbed inside the car. Peggy sat on Chloe's lap in the back seat, squashed in between Ruby and Finn. Dad switched on the radio as he started driving to the airport.

"There are just three more days until Christmas," said the radio presenter. "So here's a song to get you in a festive mood ..." A carol began to play.

"How exciting," said Dad as they drove along. "This will be Ruby's first flight."

Mine too, thought Peggy.

"I remember my first flight," said Mum. "I went to Rome on a school trip when I was sixteen."

"I'm a bit scared," said Ruby, clutching Chloe's hand.

"Don't worry," said Mum, turning around. "Flying is actually much safer than driving."

Dad came to an abrupt stop at a red light.

"Especially if Dad's driving," joked Finn.

Peggy craned her neck around. She still couldn't see any wings on her back.

They drove for a bit longer, and then Dad brought the car to a stop in front of a big building. He got their suitcases out of the boot and then hugged them each goodbye. "Have a wonderful trip," Dad said.

"Don't work too hard," said Mum, giving him a kiss.

They went inside the terminal, which was very crowded and noisy. Everyone seemed to be in a rush, and most of them were wheeling big suitcases behind them. *Where are their wings?* wondered Peggy. She stuck close to Chloe, not wanting to get stepped on.

"We need to check in," said Mum, leading them over to a desk.

A lady with a headscarf greeted them with a smile. "Where are you flying to today?" she asked them.

"Lapland," said Ruby, standing on her tiptoes to see over the counter. "That's in the north of Finland."

"How exciting," said the lady. She took their suitcases and sent them down a conveyor belt.

"Hey!" barked Peggy. "That's our stuff!"

Nobody else seemed concerned as their luggage disappeared.

"Do you want to check that in as well?" the lady asked Chloe, pointing to a carry case with mesh panels. It looked familiar to Peggy, but she couldn't remember when she'd seen it before.

"No," said Chloe. "I need it for the flight."

"You can board at Gate 7," said the lady, handing them their tickets.

"We have to go through security now," Mum told the children.

They waited in a queue and took

turns walking through an archway. When Peggy and Chloe went through, there was a beeping noise.

"Hello?" barked Peggy. *Is this some kind of creature?* she wondered.

BEEP! BEEP! BEEP! said the creature.

"Any metal objects?" asked a guard.

"Oops!" said Chloe. She unclipped Peggy's collar, which had a silver tag. Then they walked through again. This time it didn't beep.

"Phew!" said Chloe, fastening Peggy's collar back on her.

Mum checked her watch. "We have half an hour before we board. You can each choose something to read on the journey."

They went into a shop selling books, magazines and snacks. As the children browsed through the books on the shelves, Peggy looked around the shop. A man dropped a postcard into a postbox by the exit.

Peggy tugged on her lead.

"No, Peggy," said Chloe, glancing up from the book cover she was reading. "You've got to stay with me."

But Peggy remembered what Sandy the post carrier had said – it could take a few days for a letter get to Santa. She *had* to post Chloe's letter now so it reached him in time!

Yanking with all her might, Peggy broke free from Chloe's grasp and ran towards the postbox, her lead trailing behind her. She knocked over a display of books, which went flying into the air.

Peggy had nearly made it to the postbox when Chloe grabbed hold of the lead. "Naughty girl," she scolded her, picking Peggy up.

"You'd better put Peggy into her carrier before she gets up to any more mischief," said Mum.

Carrier? What carrier? thought Peggy.

Chloe put Peggy in a carry case and zipped it up. Through the mesh panel,

Peggy could see Finn, Chloe and Ruby
picking up the books she'd knocked over
and putting them back on the display.
Suddenly, Peggy remembered where she
had seen the carrier before – when she
went to the vet!

"Hey!" barked
Peggy, scrabbling
at the mesh
with her paws.
"Let me out!
I need to post
your letter!"

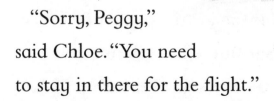

"Sorry, Peggy,"
said Chloe. "You need
to stay in there for the flight."

Oh no, thought Peggy. Now how would Santa know what Chloe wanted for Christmas? And how on earth would she be able to grow wings if she was stuck inside this thing?

Mum bought a magazine and the books the children had selected, then Chloe picked up Peggy's carry case and they walked through the airport. Peering out of her carrier, Peggy saw a long metal tube with wings.

"That's our plane!" said Chloe.

Plane? thought Peggy.

They went inside the plane and found their seats near the back. Ruby and Mum sat on one side of the aisle, Chloe and Finn on the other.

"I want the window seat," said Chloe, putting the pet carrier on her lap. "So Peggy and I can look at the clouds."

A man in a uniform came to check that their seat belts were fastened properly. "You'll need to put your dog under the seat in front of you," he said, pointing to the pet carrier.

Peggy whimpered. She wanted to see the clouds!

"It's only for a few hours, Peggy," said Chloe, lowering her to the floor.

Peggy didn't like it on the plane. It smelled funny and she couldn't see anything except for people's stinky feet.

"Welcome aboard," came the captain's voice over the speaker. "Sit back, relax and enjoy the flight."

"Here we go," said Chloe.

The plane rumbled down the runway and then Peggy felt it lift into the sky. Up, up, up they went. Peggy's ears popped as the plane climbed higher and higher. She was flying – even though she didn't have wings!

"We're here, Peggy," said Chloe a few hours later. She unfastened her seat belt and picked up Peggy's carry case.

Peggy pawed at the mesh. She couldn't wait to escape!

As soon as they got off the plane, Chloe unzipped the pet carrier and let Peggy out.

Oooh! That feels good, thought Peggy, stretching her legs.

"Look out for our suitcases," said Mum as they waited by a luggage carousel. Bags of all shapes and colours started coming out, travelling around on a conveyor belt.

There's Chloe's bag! thought Peggy, spotting a familiar purple suitcase going round. She hopped up on to the luggage carousel to get it for her friend.

WHEE! Peggy started going round with the suitcases. This was fun!

"Oh no you don't!" said Chloe, lifting Peggy – and her suitcase – down.

When everyone had collected their suitcases, they went outside and waited for a taxi.

Brrrr! Peggy shivered. Chloe had been right — it was *much* colder here. She was glad that she was wearing her new jumper.

Mum told the driver where they wanted to go, and they got inside the taxi. Leaving the airport, they drove down a long, snowy road and through a forest, then stopped in front of a cluster of pretty wooden cabins. In every window, there was a candlestick bridge glowing with light. The sign at the entrance read JOULU CABINS.

"Welcome to Lapland!" said a man with a beard, coming to greet them as they got out of the taxi. "I am your host, Timo. Who's ready to have the best Christmas ever?"

"Me!" barked Peggy, wagging her tail.

Chapter Four

Timo opened the door to their cabin. In the living room, there was a fireplace with a big basket of logs next to it and a Christmas tree decorated with lights and painted wooden ornaments.

Peggy ran around the cabin, sniffing everything. *Mmm!* She could smell fresh pine and a hint of smoke.

Above the dining table hung a
beautiful mobile made of straw.

"That's so pretty," said Chloe, staring
up at the delicate geometric shapes.

"It is a *himmeli*," said Timo. "A traditional Christmas decoration we make here in Finland." He handed Mum the key. "My family lives in the house next door. I'll give you a chance to unpack and then I will show you round. How does that sound?"

"Great!" said Mum. Turning to the children, she said, "Go put your snowsuits on."

The cabin had two bedrooms. The children were sharing a room with two bunk beds.

"I bagsie this one!" cried Finn, throwing his backpack on one of the top bunks.

"Me too," said Ruby, scrambling to the top of the other bunk.

"I guess Peggy and I are on the bottom," said Chloe.

I don't need my own bed, thought Peggy. She always slept curled up next to her best friend.

Peggy waited patiently as the children put on their boots, ski pants, parkas, hats and gloves. Then Chloe clipped on Peggy's lead and they went outside. Peggy's paws sank into the snow as they walked over to where Timo was waiting for them.

"Can Peggy come too?" asked Chloe.

"Of course," said Timo.

"Yay!" barked Peggy, bounding ahead.

"Why is the moon out already?" asked Ruby, pointing to the sky.

"Because we are near the North Pole," explained Timo. "In winter the days are short and there is very little sunlight."

Although the sun was low in the sky, it wasn't dark. The white snow reflected the moonlight, making it almost as bright as daylight. As Timo led them through the snow, Peggy could hear barking. Lots and lots of barking. *Dogs!* she thought, excited at the prospect of making some new friends.

A woman with long blonde plaits and rosy cheeks approached them with a friendly smile. "Hello. I'm Timo's wife, Johanna. Let me introduce you to our huskies."

Johanna took them past a long row of kennels. At the end there was a big pen where husky puppies were playing together. Some of the puppies rolled around in the snow, others chewed on toys and scampered over wooden ramps.

"These puppies are nearly a year old," explained Johanna. "We're training them to pull sleds. Would you like to help?"

"Yes, please!" yapped Peggy. Her family nodded eagerly.

Johanna handed everyone a harness.

"Stop wriggling," said Finn, giggling as he tried to slip his harness over a puppy's head.

"That tickles," said Ruby as a different puppy licked her face.

Chloe fastened a harness on a friendly looking puppy with bright blue eyes.

"Hi!" the puppy said to Peggy, wagging her fluffy tail. "I'm Kari.

Is your face wrinkly because you're very old?"

"No," said Peggy. "I'm Peggy. I'm actually not that much older than you."

Once all the puppies had been harnessed, Johanna showed the visitors how to attach a line to the harness.

"The puppies need to learn several commands. *Mush* means go, *haw* means turn right, *gee* means turn left – and most importantly of all, *whoa* means stop."

Mush, haw, gee, whoa, thought Peggy, memorising the instructions.

Johanna attached a tyre to the end of each puppy's line. "This is how we get

them used to pulling," she explained.
"Can I have a volunteer?"

Finn raised his hand. Johanna told
him to walk forward a few metres. Then
Finn called, "Mush!" and began to run.
His puppy chased after him and stopped
when Finn called, "Whoa!"

"Good boy," he said, rewarding the
puppy with a treat.

That looks fun, thought Peggy,
watching as Mum held her lead. She
wished she could have a go too.

Next, Chloe had her turn with Kari.

Peggy whimpered enviously as Chloe
patted Kari on the head.

"Can Peggy try?" Chloe asked.

Peggy wagged her tail and looked up at Johanna pleadingly.

"Hmm," said Johanna. "She's much smaller than the husky puppies. Let's try her out on something a bit lighter."

Johanna slipped the smallest harness over Peggy's head and fastened it so it was snug around her belly. Then she attached a line with a piece of wood at the end.

"Mush!" cried Chloe, running ahead.

Peggy chased after her friend, dragging the piece of wood behind her.

"Gee!" cried Chloe.

Peggy turned right when she was supposed to go left.

Whoops!

"Haw!" yelled Chloe.

Peggy turned left.

"Wrong way, Peggy!" shouted Ruby.

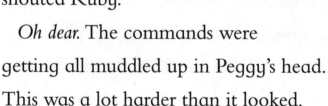

Oh dear. The commands were getting all muddled up in Peggy's head. This was a lot harder than it looked.

"Whoa!" shouted Chloe.

Panting, Peggy came to a stop.

Kari came over to Peggy and nuzzled

her nose. "Don't worry," she said. "I made lots of mistakes my first time."

Peggy nodded, too tired to reply.

"Good job!" said Chloe, giving Peggy a treat and a cuddle. "You tried really hard."

Johanna nodded approvingly. "It's important to stay positive. Sled dogs pick up on their driver's mood."

That made sense to Peggy. If Chloe was happy, she was happy too. And when her friend was upset, she felt upset too.

Peggy could feel Chloe's letter to Santa under her jumper. She had to find a way to get it to him. If Santa didn't grant Chloe's Christmas wish, her friend would be heartbroken – and so would Peggy. But she hadn't seen any postboxes out here in the woods . . .

Their lesson over, the puppies got a well-earned break. Peggy had fun frisking around in the snow with Kari and the other husky puppies.

"This is my kennel," said Kari proudly, showing Peggy a little wooden hut with straw on the floor.

"You sleep in there?" asked Peggy.

"Of course," said Kari, laughing.

"Isn't it cold?" said Peggy, thinking of Chloe's bed with its soft duvet.

"It's fine," said Kari. "Our thick fur

keeps us nice and warm."

Just then, Timo drove up on a wooden sled. It was being pulled by six grown-up huskies. The dogs were big and strong, with thick grey and white fur and long, pointy ears.

"See the dog at the front?" Kari whispered, sounding awestruck. "That's Rekku. All the other dogs have to follow him. I want to be just like Rekku when I grow up."

"This is one of our most experienced

teams," said Johanna. "They're going to Santa's workshop, ten kilometres north."

Peggy's ears pricked up at the mention of Santa. Maybe the huskies could help her.

"Don't the dogs get tired?" asked Chloe, looking concerned.

"Huskies are very strong," said Johanna. "We take very good care of them and give them lots of good food so they have plenty of energy."

"Salmon's my favourite dinner," Kari told Peggy. "It's yummy!"

"Can we go for a sled ride too?" asked Ruby.

"I'm afraid all of our sled rides are

fully booked today," said Timo.

"Aw," said Ruby as a mother and her little boy climbed into the sled.

"Hi, Rekku!" Kari called to the big dog at the front of the team. She jumped up and down excitedly, trying to get the lead dog's attention. "This is my new friend, Peggy."

Rekku looked Peggy up and down scornfully. "Who are you? Why are your legs so short?"

"I'm a pug," Peggy explained. "My legs are supposed to look like this. I'm visiting with my family."

"You're a *pet*," sneered Rekku. He said it like it was something terrible.

Peggy was proud of being Chloe's pet. She would do anything to help her friend.

"Are you really going to Santa's workshop?" Peggy asked the big husky.

"Yes," Rekku said coldly, looking

down his long nose at her.

"Could you please deliver a letter to him for me?" said Peggy. She pictured the disappointment on Chloe's face if Dad wasn't with them for Christmas.

"I don't have time for that nonsense," said Rekku. "Now get out of my way."

"Mush!" cried Timo.

"Let's go!" barked Rekku. The husky surged forward, his muscles straining against the harness. The other dogs followed his lead, their paws scrabbling over the snow as they ran.

"Bye!" Kari called after them.

"Please!" wailed Peggy desperately, watching them go. "I need to help

Chloe!" But the dog sled disappeared down the snowy trail, and with it, Peggy's hopes of getting Chloe's letter to Santa.

Chapter Five

"What should we do today?" asked
Mum as they ate breakfast the next
morning. A pile of brochures and
leaflets were spread out on the table.
Peggy's family studied them in between
mouthfuls of porridge and smoked
salmon on brown rye bread.

"I want to go ski jumping," said Finn, picking up a leaflet with a picture of a steep slope on it.

"That sounds a bit dangerous," said Mum. She sipped her coffee. "We could go cross-country skiing instead. I hear that's very good exercise."

"Sounds boring," said Finn, wrinkling his nose.

"What about visiting a reindeer farm," suggested Chloe, studying a brochure with a picture of a reindeer on it.

"I'd rather visit Santa Claus," said Ruby.

"Here, Peggy," said Chloe, tossing her a piece of something pink. "Try some of this delicious salmon."

Peggy gobbled it down and discovered that Kari was right. Salmon was yummy!

There was a knock on the cabin door. Peggy barked, just in case her family hadn't heard it. Mum answered the door. Timo stood outside with two blonde children about the same age as Finn and Chloe.

"Good morning!" he said. "These are my children, Jasper and Elin." The boy and girl gave a little wave. They were each holding a pair of ice skates. "We wondered if you might like to come ice skating with us."

Mum turned back to the kids. "What
do you say, gang?"

The children nodded enthusiastically.

"Yes, please!" said Chloe.

"Yay!" said Ruby. "I've never been ice
skating before!"

"You'll soon pick it up," said Finn.

Peggy hadn't been ice skating either.

She hoped it was easier than pulling a dog sled.

Finn and Chloe fetched their skates. As she put on an extra pair of woolly socks, Ruby said, "I wonder what Daddy is doing today?"

"Working, I expect," said Finn, wrapping a scarf around his neck.

"Dad loves ice skating," said Chloe. "I wish he could be here with us."

Peggy thought of the letter tucked under her jumper. Time was running out to post it to Santa . . .

I need to be an elf, thought Peggy, remembering the story Dad had read them. She would just have to deliver the letter to Santa herself.

When they were all bundled up in warm clothes, they met Timo and his kids outside. As they walked to the ice rink, their boots crunching on the snow, the children quickly made friends with Elin and Jasper.

"I don't have skates," said Ruby.

Neither do I, thought Peggy.

"You can hire some at the rink," said Elin.

The ice rink was outdoors, surrounded by twinkling Christmas trees and ice sculptures shaped like reindeer, snowmen, elves and – of course – Santa Claus. There were little huts around the rink selling refreshments. Peggy sniffed the air. *Gingerbread,* she thought, recognising the smell.

"Hey, look," said Chloe. "*Piparkakku!*"

"You speak Finnish!" said Elin.

"I don't," said Chloe, laughing. "That's the only word I know."

"Then let me teach you another one," said Jasper. "*Luistin.*"

"What does that mean?" asked Finn.

Elin held up her skate. "It means ice skate!"

Mum went over to a hut and hired a pair of ice skates for Ruby. When she returned, Chloe said, "Now let's go put our *luistins* on!"

"Actually," said Jasper, "It's *luistimet* when there's more than one of them."

Mum helped Ruby lace up her skates.

Where are mine? wondered Peggy.

"Come on, Rubes," said Chloe, taking her little sister's hand and leading her on to the ice. "I'll show you what to do."

Peggy tried to follow them on to the rink but Mum picked her up. "Sorry, Pegs. You've got to stay with me."

No fair, thought Peggy. Ice skating looked fun.

Ruby clung nervously to the side as Chloe skated gracefully around the rink. She came to a stop in front of Ruby. "Now you try."

Ruby let go of the side and pushed off with her right skate. She glided across the ice then started to wobble. Her arms windmilled around wildly and a moment later – BUMP! – she landed on her bottom.

"Ow!" Ruby wailed.

Oh dear, thought Peggy. Ruby didn't have a tail to cushion her fall.

Chloe helped Ruby get back up. "Everyone falls over when they're learning to skate," she told her sister. "You've just got to keep trying."

"This will help you balance," said Finn, skating over with a big plastic penguin with handles to hold on to.

Soon, Ruby was happily pushing the penguin around the rink. Peggy watched the children glide across the ice. Finn practised skating backwards while Chloe tried balancing on one leg. Jasper and Elin were both really good – they could even do spins and jumps! Peggy watched them go round so many times she started to feel dizzy.

There was an announcement over the speakers. Everyone came off the ice and gathered around the edge of the rink.

"What's going on?" Chloe asked Elin.

"The local skating team is putting on a show," explained Timo. He went over to a hut selling refreshments and came back with a tray of hot chocolate and gingerbread shaped like hearts.

The children gathered around the edge of the rink, sipping their hot chocolate and nibbling gingerbread hearts as they waited for the performance to begin.

"I like *piparkakku*," said Chloe, breaking off a piece and feeding it to Peggy.

Peggy gulped it down. *Yum!* She liked it too!

Music began to play and a couple skated on to the ice. The man was dressed as a soldier and the woman wore a floaty pink dress.

Chloe picked Peggy up so she could see the skaters. "He's the Nutcracker Prince and she's the Sugar Plum Fairy," explained Chloe.

Peggy watched in awe as the pair danced across the ice, performing daring lifts.

Oooh! everyone gasped as they finished their routine with a gravity-defying jump.

Next, a team of girls dressed in fur-trimmed elf dresses stepped into the rink. Skating in perfect unison, they formed a star shape on the ice. They skated in formation, making the star spin around and around.

"They're really good," said Chloe.

A man with a white beard and a red costume joined them on the ice for a solo. He whizzed around the rink, doing athletic jumps and splits in the air.

Santa! thought Peggy. This was her chance to give him Chloe's letter!

Wriggling out of Chloe's arms, Peggy jumped on to the ice. Her paws slipped and skidded as she tried to run across it.

"No, Peggy!" shouted Chloe. "Come back!"

Normally Peggy obeyed Chloe, but this was too important.

"Santa!" she barked. "I have something for you!"

Whoops! Peggy's paws shot out from underneath her and she slid across the ice on her curly tail like a hockey puck. Going too fast to stop, Peggy crashed into the elf skaters, who toppled over like a line of dominoes.

"Sorry!" barked Peggy, scrambling back on to her paws. She ran towards Santa, who swerved to avoid her and – THUMP! – crashed into the side of the rink. He landed flat on his back.

"I need to talk to you, Santa!" Peggy
barked. "It's really important!"

As Santa sat up, his white beard fell off. The face underneath it was young. *Uh oh* . . . Peggy suddenly realised that he wasn't really Santa at all.

"I'm so sorry," said Chloe, hurrying on to the ice to collect Peggy.

"It's OK," said the Santa skater. "The show was almost over."

Luckily, Peggy's family weren't cross with her either.

"That was so funny," said Finn, chuckling.

"Peggy is even worse at ice skating than me," said Ruby.

"Too bad Dad didn't get to see it," said Chloe.

Peggy heard the sadness in her friend's voice and it made her heart ache too. She still hadn't delivered Chloe's letter and tomorrow was Christmas Eve. She was running out of time to make sure her friend's wish came true!

Chapter Six

"Mmm," said Mum, taking a freshly baked batch of gingerbread out of the oven. "These look delicious."

It was snowing outside, so they'd decided to stay in and bake *piparkakku* using a recipe Johanna had given them. Peggy was sitting by the roaring fire.

Chloe bit into one of the hearts that was cooling on a tray. "They taste really good too."

"We can leave some out for Santa," said Ruby.

"You'd better make another batch," said Mum, laughing. "I don't think these will last very long."

Finn mixed up the ingredients in a bowl, Chloe rolled out the dough and Ruby cut out hearts.

"I thought I'd make a traditional Finnish Christmas Eve dinner tonight," said Mum.

"What's that?" asked Chloe.

"Baked ham, cabbage, root vegetable

casserole . . ." said Mum.

"Yum," said Finn.

". . . and pickled herring," continued Mum.

"Yuck!" said Ruby.

"You should try it," said Mum. "You might like it."

Normally, all this talk of food would make Peggy hungry. But today she felt too worried to eat. She still hadn't delivered Chloe's letter to Santa.

"*Maaaaaaaa! Maaaaaaa!*" The sound of bleating came from outside. Peggy ran to the window and put her front paws on the sill. A shaggy animal with curly horns and a long beard was standing outside the cabin.

What type of dog is that? wondered Peggy.

"Mum!" called Chloe, joining Peggy at the window. "There's a goat outside our cabin!"

Mum opened the front door. Suddenly,

four people wearing masks and costumes jumped out from behind a pine tree and began to sing. The two tall ones were dressed as elves, and the two smaller ones were disguised as a reindeer and an angel.

When they finished, they lifted their masks and Peggy saw four faces she recognised. Timo and Johanna were the elves, Elin was the angel and Jasper was the reindeer.

"What's all this?" asked Mum, laughing.

"We are *julebukking*," said Timo, tying the goat up to a tree. "It is a tradition to go door to door on Christmas Eve, singing carols to our neighbours."

"So they give us candy!" said Elin, grinning.

"That's like when we go trick or treating at Halloween," said Chloe.

"I don't have any candy," said Mum. "But I *can* offer you some freshly baked gingerbread." She invited them inside and passed round a plate of gingerbread hearts.

"What's up with the goat?" asked Finn.

"It's another Christmas tradition," explained Jasper. "We play pranks on our friends and family – like bringing a Yule goat to their house."

"That's hilarious," said Finn, chuckling.

"It belongs to my friend," said Elin. "Her family lives on a farm."

"What does Yule mean?" asked Ruby.

"It's another word for Christmas," said Mum.

"Back in the days when Santa Claus was still called Saint Nicholas," explained Timo, "he had a Yule goat instead of reindeer."

Peggy looked at the goat standing out in the cold. Maybe he would be able to tell her how to get to Santa! She whined and scratched the door, so Mum let her go out.

"Hello," Peggy said to the goat. "Do you know how to get to Santa's workshop?"

"Of course I do," he said. "I am a Yule goat. We used to pull his sleigh."

"Why did Santa switch to reindeer?" asked Peggy. "Are they faster?"

"*Maaaaaahhh!*" bleated the goat indignantly. "Reindeer! That's all anyone cares about these days. I suppose you think a Yule goat is just a joke."

Oh dear. She hadn't meant to offend him. "I'm sorry. Can you take me to see Santa? I've got to give him something important."

Just then, Timo and his family came out of the cabin. He untied the goat. "We'd better go play a prank on our other neighbours."

"Wait!" Peggy called after the goat as it started trotting off. "Can you tell me how to get to Santa's workshop?"

"Why don't you ask a *reindeer,*" the goat shot back.

"Come back inside, Peggy," called Chloe. "It's cold out here."

Peggy went indoors reluctantly. The goat knew how to get to Santa – but she'd blown her chances. Disappointed, Peggy flopped down on the floor, wracking her brain for a new plan.

Mum went back to the kitchen to finish making the last batch of gingerbread and Finn went into the bedroom to read. The girls sat in front of the fire, wrapping up the presents for Timo, Johanna, Jasper and Elin that they'd bought at the Christmas market

yesterday. Chloe cut out a piece of
wrapping paper, while Ruby handed
her pieces of sticky tape.

Peggy wanted to help too. She tugged
a piece of sticky tape with her teeth.
She tried to break it off with her paws,
but they got stuck.

She rolled
around,
waving her
paws, trying
to get the
tape off her,
but more and
more kept coming off the reel. Soon, she
was all tangled up in sticky tape, with

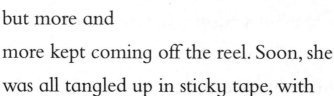

bits of wrapping paper stuck to her.

"Help!" Peggy yelped.

"Silly Peggy," said Chloe. She gently removed the sticky tape from Peggy's paws and fur.

"I've got an idea . . ." Chloe whispered, her eyes twinkling mischievously. She took a small piece of clear tape and used it to stick the light switch down.

"What are you doing?" asked Ruby.

"Wait and see," replied Chloe mysteriously.

When Finn came into the room, Chloe said, "Can you turn on the light, please."

Finn went over and tried to switch the

light on. "What the—"

The girls burst out laughing.

"Gotcha!" Chloe said.

"We played a Christmas prank on you," said Ruby, giggling.

Rolling his eyes, Finn went into the kitchen. A few minutes later, he called, "Come quick!"

Peggy followed the girls as they ran into the kitchen. Finn pointed to a brown splat on the floor. "Peggy had an accident."

"Oh no!" said Chloe.

"Gross!" said Ruby, holding her nose.

I most certainly did not have an accident! Peggy was horrified by the suggestion.

She hadn't pooped on the floor since she was a tiny puppy!

"I'd better clean it up," said Finn. He picked the brown blob up with his bare hands . . . and threw it at Chloe!

"Ew!" she shrieked.

Finn clutched his sides as he laughed. "I can't believe you fell for that! It's not dog poo, it's gingerbread dough!"

"Don't be disgusting," said Mum, taking the blob of dough off Finn and dropping it in the bin.

Finn left the kitchen, chuckling.

"We've got to get him back," said Chloe. She went to the refrigerator and took out a cabbage. Giggling, she and

Ruby took it to the living room and wrapped it up.

"Oh Finn!" Ruby sang. "There's a present for you under the tree."

"It looks like a football," said Chloe, winking at her sister.

"Awesome," said Finn. "I need a new one." He ripped off the wrapping paper

– and found the cabbage inside.

"We got you!" cried Ruby, jumping up and down.

"Enough pranks," said Mum, taking the cabbage before Finn could throw it at his sister. "At this rate we won't have anything left for Christmas dinner."

Ruby and Chloe went back to wrapping presents.

"I hear bells," said Finn.

"Ha ha," said Chloe. "Very funny." She didn't even bother to look up.

"No, I'm serious," said Finn.

Peggy's ears pricked up. She could hear a jingling sound too.

Finn went over to the window and

pulled back the curtain. "There's a dog sled outside!" he said.

"Yeah right," said Chloe. "I'm not falling for another one of your pranks."

"Why don't you check," said Mum. "Just to be sure."

Peggy and the girls went over to the window. Chloe gasped. There *was* a dog sled waiting outside!

"Is that for us?" asked Ruby.

"Yes," said Mum. "I arranged it with Timo earlier."

"This isn't a Christmas prank?" said Chloe, her eyes wide.

Mum smiled. "It isn't a prank. Get ready, everybody – we're going on a sled ride to Santa's workshop!"

Yes! thought Peggy, her heart leaping with excitement. She was finally going to be able to deliver Chloe's letter!

Chapter Seven

Outside, the huskies barked and pawed
the snow, eager to be on their way.
It was still snowing as Chloe carried
Peggy out to the sled. A fluffy flake
landed on Peggy's nose and she licked
it off.

As the children climbed into the sled,

Peggy greeted the big dog in the lead. "Hello, Rekku," she said.

"Oh, it's the little pet," he sniffed. "Real dogs don't ride in sleds, they pull them."

I am a real dog, thought Peggy, curling up on Chloe's lap in the fur-lined sled. Not even Rekku's rude remark could spoil her excitement at finally getting to deliver the letter to Santa.

Johanna was standing on the back of the sled. She stepped off, letting Mum take her place. She showed her how to step on the brake to slow the sled down. Then she crouched down to talk to the kids. "Lean your weight in the opposite direction to the way the dogs are turning," she told them. "That keeps the sled balanced and stops it from rolling over."

"How do I know which way to go?" Mum asked her.

"Just follow the signs along the path," said Johanna. "Head north and you'll get to Santa's workshop in about an hour." She gave Mum her number. "Call me if you need help."

"Yay!" cried Ruby.

"We're going to see Santa, Peggy!" said Chloe, cuddling her.

Peggy wagged her tail excitedly. Now it didn't matter that Chloe hadn't posted her letter to Santa – she could tell him her Christmas wish herself!

"Mush!" cried Mum.

The children jerked backwards as the dogs raced down a path lined with pine trees. Snow stung Peggy's face and the wind blew her jowls and ears back as they whizzed over the snow.

"Whee!" cried Chloe, gripping the side of the sled.

"This is so fun!" shouted Ruby.

"Woo hoo!" called Finn.

The dogs ran tirelessly, their pace never slowing.

"Haw!" called Mum as the path curved to the right.

The dogs turned right, so the children leaned to the left.

"Gee!" called Mum as they approached another bend.

Rekku turned left, and the whole team followed his lead. They had been travelling for nearly an hour, across the snowy wilderness, when one of the dogs stumbled and yelped in pain.

"Whoa!" said Mum, bringing the sled to a halt.

Oh no, thought Peggy. She jumped off Chloe's lap and ran over to the howling husky.

Mum unfastened the dog's harness and stroked his fur to comfort him. "He's hurt his leg," she said.

Peggy could see the pain in the dog's eyes. "Don't worry," she told him. "My family will help you."

Finn helped Mum carry the injured husky to the sled. Then Mum took out her phone. "I guess I'll have to call Johanna to come and get us. Sorry guys, we won't get to visit Santa's workshop after all."

"No!" barked Peggy. She *had* to get Chloe to Santa! "I can help!" She pawed the injured dog's harness.

"I think Peggy wants to pull the sled," said Chloe.

"She's much too little," said Mum.

"Let her try," said Chloe. "She knows what to do."

As Mum and Ruby comforted the injured dog, Chloe put the harness on Peggy. It was far too big, so she tightened the straps to make it fit. Then Peggy took her place at the front of the sled next to Rekku.

"You really think you can do this?" the lead husky said, looking doubtful.

"Yes," said Peggy. She was determined to make sure Chloe had a happy Christmas.

"Mush!" shouted Mum.

Peggy strained on her harness, but nothing happened. The sled was much heavier than she'd expected it to be.

"What a surprise," said Rekku sarcastically. "The little pet isn't up to the job."

But Peggy wasn't going to give up.

"Mush!" Mum called again.

"You can do it, Peggy!" cheered Chloe. "I believe in you."

Peggy's heart swelled with love. *I can do it,* she thought. *I can do it for Chloe.* She tried again, pulling with every bit of strength she possessed. This time the sled began to slide forward.

"Keep going," barked Rekku.

Peggy's paws flew along the path, barely touching the snow. Her short legs were half the size of the huskies', so she had to run twice as fast to keep up with them. Her heart was pounding hard, her breath coming out in puffs, but she knew she couldn't stop.

It was nearly evening and the full moon shone bright in the clear sky. If they didn't get to Santa's workshop soon, they would miss him. He and his reindeer would have already set off on their journey around the world.

Faster, Peggy told herself. Summoning all the energy she had left, she made her legs move even faster.

"There it is!" cried Ruby from the sled. "Santa's workshop!"

In the distance, Peggy could see a wooden building that looked like a life-sized gingerbread house. It had a pointed roof and red and white striped pillars that looked like candy canes.

With one last burst of speed, Peggy and the rest of the huskies pulled the sled to the building.

"We made it!" said Chloe.

Phew! thought Peggy. Panting, she collapsed in the snow. It was very cold, but she was too tired to care.

"You did well," said Rekku, putting his big paw gently over her small one. "I'm sorry I called you a pet."

"I *am* a pet," said Peggy as Chloe unfastened her harness. "And there's nothing wrong with that."

"Oh Peggy," said Chloe, giving her a cuddle. "I am so proud of you."

Peggy licked her best friend's cheek.

An elf with pointy ears and a hat with a bell on the end of it came out to meet them. "Hello," he said. "I'm Jingle. Welcome to Santa's workshop."

Mum explained about the husky with the injured leg.

"One of the other elves is a vet," Jingle said. "He specialises in looking after reindeer, but I'm sure he will take good care of your dog."

Jingle fetched the vet elf, then took Mum, Peggy and the children into the workshop.

"There's so much going on!" said Finn, gazing around in astonishment.

"Yes," said Jingle. "It's our busiest night of the year."

The workshop was a hive of activity. Some elves were making toys, others were wrapping presents and still others bustled around packing the gifts into a big red sack. No matter how many they put in, there always seemed to be room for more presents.

"Can we meet Santa?" asked Ruby.

"I'm afraid Santa is busy checking his list right now," said Jingle.

"His list?" asked Finn.

"The Naughty or Nice list," explained Jingle. "He always checks it twice, just to be on the safe side." He smiled at the children. "But I'm sure you three are all on the nice list."

"So we can't meet Santa?" asked Chloe, looking as if she was about to cry.

"I'm afraid not," said Jingle.

No! thought Peggy. This couldn't be happening. How was Chloe going to tell Santa her wish?

"I can give you a tour of the workshop," said Jingle. "And afterwards we'll have hot chocolate with Mrs Claus."

Jingle brought Peggy's family over to a workbench, where elves were carving wooden blocks and painting faces on dolls with pink dresses.

"Quickly!" said the elf in charge.

"It's nearly time for Santa to leave!"

"There are always a few children who don't post their letters on time," explained Jingle with a sigh. "So we're dealing with some last-minute requests."

But what about Chloe? worried Peggy. She hadn't posted her letter at all. It was still tucked under Peggy's jumper.

"Let's move on to the gift wrap department," said Jingle. He led them over to a room filled with rolls of shiny wrapping paper, and reels of ribbon in every colour.

I've got to do something, thought Peggy. Santa was busy – but he had to be nearby. If only there was some way

of getting to him, she could give him
Chloe's letter. She slipped away from
the group. When nobody was looking,
Peggy jumped into the big red sack and
landed on something squishy. It was too
dark in the bag for Peggy to see much,
but it felt like a teddy bear.

"OK, this is the last
one," she heard an
elf say.

A moment
later, a gift
wrapped in
gold paper was
dropped into the
sack, clonking her

right on the head.

Ouch! Peggy winced and rubbed her head with her paw. The gift was something hard – the wooden blocks, she guessed. She didn't cry out because she didn't want to be discovered.

"Take Santa's sack out to the stables," said the elf.

Peggy felt the sack being lifted up. A rush of cold air told her she was being taken outside. A few minutes later, the sack was set down again.

Peggy wriggled her way to the top of the sack of presents and peeped out. Her plan had worked! She was in a sleigh. A man with a big white beard, a red coat

and black boots was harnessing eight
reindeer to the sleigh.

Santa! thought Peggy. She could tell
from the twinkle in his eye that it was
really him this time.

"Fly well tonight, Dasher," he said,
patting the reindeer. Dasher nodded,
making the silver bells on her leather
harness jingle.

"Santa!" Peggy barked, jumping
out of the sack. "I have something to
deliver!"

"Ho ho ho!" chuckled Santa. "I don't
remember anyone asking for a pug for
Christmas. My elves must be playing a
prank on me."

"No!" said Peggy. "I'm not a prank!"
Climbing into the sleigh, Santa picked
Peggy up. "Aren't you a cutie," he said.
"You look like a little elf."

Santa reached his hand under her jumper to tickle her belly. "I say . . . What's this?" Frowning, he pulled out Chloe's letter.

"It's for you!" barked Peggy excitedly.

Taking a pair of spectacles out of his red coat, Santa perched them on his nose. Then he unfolded the letter and began to read . . .

Chapter Eight

Hurrah, thought Peggy as Santa read Chloe's letter. Santa was magical – he had a team of flying reindeer and could get around the world in one night. Peggy was sure he could grant Chloe's Christmas wish.

Santa folded up the letter. "We'll

soon be on our way," he told the reindeer, who were pawing the ground impatiently. Picking Peggy up, he climbed out of the sleigh and carried her back into the workshop.

"Is anyone missing a dog?" he asked.

"Santa!" cried Ruby and Finn.

"Peggy!" exclaimed Chloe.

Peggy jumped down from Santa's arms and ran to Chloe, wagging her curly tail.

"We were looking everywhere for you, Peggy," said Chloe. She picked Peggy up and kissed her on the head. "I thought we'd lost you."

"Are you Chloe?" said Santa, smiling

kindly.

"Yes," said Chloe.

"Peggy gave me your letter," said Santa. "You want your dad to spend Christmas with you."

"He couldn't come with us," said Chloe sadly. "He had to work."

"I can tell how much you love him," said Santa. "And I know he loves you very much too. But it's already Christmas Eve, so I'm not sure there's much even I can do."

Chloe bit her lip. Peggy could tell she was trying hard not to cry. She nuzzled Chloe's nose, trying to comfort her.

Santa put his hand on Chloe's shoulder. "Many families can't be together at Christmastime, Chloe," he said. "But that doesn't mean they aren't in each other's hearts."

Chloe nodded bravely.

Santa beckoned Jingle over and whispered in his ear. The elf hurried off and returned a few minutes later holding a stack of parcels.

"This will save me from making a stop," said Santa. He handed Finn a rectangular box with a green bow.

Finn opened the present and took out a pair of red and black football boots. "Wicked!" he said with a grin.

Santa looked puzzled.

"That means very good, Santa," explained Jingle.

"This one's for Ruby," said Santa.

Ruby tore her gift open eagerly and found a pair of white ice skates with gleaming silver blades inside.

"Just what I wanted!" she said. She threw her arms around Santa's big belly. "Thank you so much!"

Finally, Santa handed Chloe a gift. "I know it's not quite what you wanted," said Santa. "But I hope you like it."

Chloe opened her present. It was a board game. "Thanks," she said quietly. "It looks really fun."

"You can play it with Dad when we get back home," said Mum.

Santa hadn't forgotten Mum and Peggy, either. Mum got a bottle of perfume, and Peggy got a chew toy shaped like a candy cane.

Santa glanced at the clock on the wall. It was nearly six o'clock. "Well, I should be setting off," he told them. "I've got a long night ahead of me, and the reindeer will be wanting some carrots."

Before he left, he reached into his pocket and took out a bell. His eyes

twinkled
merrily
as he
attached it
to Peggy's
collar.
"A bit of
Christmas
magic
to help
you on the
journey home," he

whispered in her ear.

"Bye, Santa," called Finn.

"Have a safe trip," said Ruby.

"Thank you for our gifts," said Chloe.

She was smiling bravely, but Peggy knew how disappointed her friend must feel.

Once Santa had gone back to the stables, Peggy and her family had hot chocolate and bowls of rice pudding with Mrs Claus and the elves.

"This is what we always serve on Christmas Eve," explained Mrs Claus. She wore a white apron over her red dress, and her white hair was in a bun.

"Mmm," said Mum, taking a bite. "It's delicious. I can't quite place what spice you've added."

"It's a pinch of Christmas magic," said Mrs Claus, winking. She went over to the stove and ladled out another bowl of rice pudding. "You must be hungry too, dear," said Mrs Claus, setting the bowl on the floor for Peggy.

Yum! Peggy gobbled up the rice pudding. As she licked the bowl clean, her teeth crunched something hard.

"I think Peggy found the almond," said Mrs Claus.

"Mine didn't have any almonds," said Chloe.

"There's only one. That's the tradition here. Whoever finds the almond in the rice pudding gets to make a wish," explained Mrs Claus.

"I bet Peggy will wish for sausages,"

joked Finn. "Those are her favourite treat."

Peggy did love sausages. But she loved Chloe even more.

I wish Dad could spend Christmas with us, thought Peggy.

When they'd all finished their rice pudding, they went back out to the sled, where the huskies were waiting. The vet elf had fed the dogs and put the injured husky's leg in a splint.

"He'll soon be as good as new," the elf told them. "But he needs to stay off it for a while."

"It's a long way back to the cabin," said Mum. "I'm not sure Peggy can make it all that way."

"Yes, I can!" barked Peggy. She wasn't
sure if it was the rice pudding or the
fact that she'd had a rest, but she was
raring to go.

Chloe fastened Peggy's harness. As the
children climbed into the sled with their
gifts, Peggy took her place at the front,
next to Rekku.

"You're back," said the husky. "Did
you deliver your letter?"

"Yes," Peggy said.

"Mush!" shouted Mum.

Peggy and the huskies began to
run, pulling the sled. The silver bell on
Peggy's collar jingled merrily as she

raced home. Thanks to Santa's magic, she didn't feel even a tiny bit tired! Her feet seemed to fly effortlessly over the snow.

In the distance, she could see the cabin, the lights in the window glowing invitingly. As the sled got closer, Peggy noticed someone sitting on the step, waiting for them. He was wearing a snowflake sweater, just like the ones the rest of Peggy's family were wearing.

"Dad!" shouted Chloe. "It's Dad!"

Peggy's heart leaped with joy. Chloe's Christmas wish had come true!

"Whoa!" called Mum, bringing the sled to a stop.

Chloe jumped out of the sled and ran
over to her father.

"You came!" she said happily, hugging
him tight.

"I finished my work earlier than expected," said Dad. "So I caught the last flight out here." He gave everyone else a hug.

"We met Santa," said Ruby.

"And the elves," said Chloe.

Johanna came over and Mum explained about the injured dog. Then she unfastened Peggy's harness.

"Happy Christmas, Rekku," Peggy said to the big husky.

"I was wrong about you," growled Rekku. "If you ever want to be a sled dog, I'd be honoured to have you on my team. You would be a great leader."

"Thanks," said Peggy. "But I like

being a pet. I'm happy just being me."

"I'd better get these guys back in their kennels," said Johanna, leading the dogs away.

As they walked towards the cabin, holding their gifts from Santa, Chloe gasped and pointed to the sky. "Look!" she said.

"The aurora borealis!" said Finn.

Peggy stared up in amazement as green and purple lights swirled and twirled across the night sky. She had never seen anything so beautiful.

"I guess I timed my visit perfectly," said Dad.

As they stood outside, gazing up at

the northern lights dancing in the sky, Peggy caught a glimpse of something even more magical – Santa's sleigh silhouetted against the moon!

Thanks, Santa, thought Peggy as the reindeers' bells jingled in the night. She sighed contentedly. Santa had worked his magic and granted Chloe's wish. The whole family was together again, just in time for Christmas.

"Let's go inside and light a fire," said Ruby, tugging on Dad's hand.

"You can taste our gingerbread," said Finn.

"And play my new game," said Chloe.

"I can't wait!" said Dad, grinning.

Putting his arm around Mum, he went inside the cabin.

Chloe picked up Peggy and kissed her on the head. "This is definitely the best Christmas ever, Peggy!" she said happily.

WOOF! barked Peggy, her tail wagging. She could not have agreed more!

The End

Have you read all of Peggy the pug's adventures?

The Pug *who wanted to be a* Unicorn

Bella Swift

The Pug *who wanted to be a* Reindeer

Bella Swift

The Pug *who wanted to be a* Bunny

Bella Swift

The Pug *who wanted to be a* Pumpkin

Bella Swift

The Pug *who wanted to be a* Mermaid

Bella Swift

The Pug *who wanted to be a* Star

Bella Swift

The Pug *who wanted to be a* Fairy

Bella Swift

The Pug *who wanted to be an* Elf

Bella Swift